A Bunch of Daisies

To all the children and staff of Pelican Place – KG
For Fran – NS

A BUNCH OF DAISIES
A RED FOX BOOK 978 0 099 44803 7

First published in Great Britain by The Bodley Head,
an imprint of Random House Children's Publishers UK

The Bodley Head edition published 2005
Red Fox edition published 2006

9 10 8

Set in Lemonade

Red Fox Books are published by Random House Children's Publishers UK
61–63 Uxbridge Road, London W5 5SA,
a division of The Random House Group Ltd.
Addresses for companies within The Random House Group Limited can be found at : www.randomhouse,.co.uk/offices.htm

THE RANDOM HOUSE GROUP Limited Reg. No. 954009
www.randomhousechildrens.co.uk

A CIP catalogue record for this book is available from the British Library.

Printed and bound in China

A Bunch of Daisies

Kes Gray & Nick Sharratt

RED FOX

Crunchy Cream

"Can I have a biscuit?" asked Daisy, picking up the biscuit tin.

"Pardon?" said Daisy's *mum*.

"PLEASE can I have a biscuit?" asked Daisy, pulling off the lid.

"You can have ONE," said Daisy's *mum*, looking under
the cushions on the sofa. "You don't want to spoil
your appetite."

Daisy peered inside the biscuit tin.
It was full to the top with biscuits. But the biscuit
Daisy wanted was buried out of sight. She had seen it there
the night before when her *mum* was refilling the tin.

 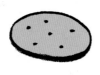    

"Have you seen the car keys, Daisy?" asked her *mum*, poking her hands down the back of the sofa. "I can't find them anywhere."

"No," said Daisy, pushing her fingers deep into the biscuit tin to find the crunchy cream.

"Don't put your fingers through the biscuits, Daisy," said her *mum*, emptying out her handbag.

"If you want a biscuit, take one from the top."

Daisy pulled her fingers out of the biscuits and sighed. She didn't want a biscuit from the top, she wanted the crunchy cream at the bottom.

 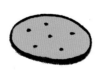   

"Maybe I can shake the crunchy cream to the top," thought Daisy, replacing the lid and giving the biscuit tin a good shake.

"Don't shake them, you'll break them!" said her mum, rummaging through the coat pockets in the hallway.

"Maybe I can wish the crunchy cream to the top," thought Daisy, closing her eyes and hugging the biscuit tin tightly.

She opened her eyes, removed the lid and peered inside the tin.

The crunchy cream was still buried.

"Maybe I can washing-machine the crunchy cream to the top," thought Daisy, walking into the kitchen and placing the biscuit tin on top of the washing machine.

She watched as the washing machine wobbled and vibrated its way through a spin cycle before coming to a shuddery, juddery stop. Daisy picked up the biscuit tin and looked inside. There was still no sign of the crunchy cream.

"Are you sure you haven't seen the car keys, Daisy?" asked her mum, looking down the back of the microwave.

Daisy shook her head and stared into the biscuit tin.
She had completely run out of ideas.

 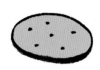    

Daisy's mum had run out of ideas too.

"C'mon, Daisy! Think!" she said. "Think where the car keys might be!"

Daisy put the biscuit tin down on the kitchen table and thought. She thought and thought her very hardest and then smiled.

"I think I know where I might have seen them," she said.

"Where?" asked her mum.

"In the biscuit tin," said Daisy.

Daisy's mum snatched up the biscuit tin and tipped all the biscuits out onto the table.

"No, they're not in there," sighed Daisy's mum.

"Mmm, but the crunchy cream is!" munched Daisy.

Colours I've Invented

PILLOW (pink with yellow)

GRUE (green with blue)

BRED (brown with red)

BLEEN (black with green)

RELLOW (red with yellow)

BLINK (black with pink)

BOGYPOP (BlackOrangeGreenYellowPurple and a bit more orange and some pink)

Floppyitis

Daisy had floppyitis.

Not all the time. Just here and there, now and then.

When her mum asked her to pick her clothes up

off the bedroom floor, Daisy's arms

went all floppy and

she couldn't pick

anything up at all.

When her *mum* asked her to help unpack the shopping, Daisy's wrists went all floppy and she couldn't even pick up a yoghurt pot.

When her *mum* asked her to put her empty crisp packet in the wastepaper basket, Daisy's bottom went so floppy, she couldn't even get up off the sofa.

Now that it was time for Daisy to go to bed, her legs had gone so floppy, she couldn't even climb up the first step.

"I hope floppyitis isn't catching," smiled Daisy's *mum*, carrying Daisy up the stairs.

"Please will *you* read *me* a bedtime story?"

asked Daisy, flopping into bed.

"OK," said her *mum*, taking a book down from the shelf.

"Once upon a flop, there floppa flopfloppa flopflop . . .
I'm sorry, Daisy," said Mum, "my tongue has gone all floppy.
I can't possibly read you a story with floppyitis."

"Can I have a good-night kiss?" asked Daisy.

"It will have to be a floppy one," said Daisy's *mum*.

The next morning, Daisy went out to play in her garden.
When her ball went over the wall, she asked her neighbour
if she could please throw it back.

"I'm sorry, Daisy," said her neighbour, "my fingers have gone
all floppy. I must have floppyitis. I can't possibly throw
your ball back."

That afternoon, Daisy's granddad took her to the park.

"Will you push me on the swings please, Granddad?"
asked Daisy.

"I'm sorry, Daisy," said her granddad, "my arms have gone
all floppy. I must have floppyitis, too. I can't possibly push
you on the swings."

When Daisy got home she flopped out on a chair in the kitchen. She thought about things for a few moments then sat up straight.

"Mum," she said, "my flops have stopped. I haven't got floppyitis any more."

Daisy's *mum* smiled and handed Daisy a pen and paper. "That's good news, Daisy! Now you can finally write your birthday thank-you letters!"

Daisy flopped onto the floor.

"My floppyitis has just come back," she groaned.

Animals From Underneath

Can you guess what animals these are?

1.

2.

3.

4.

5.

6.

8.

7.

9.

10.

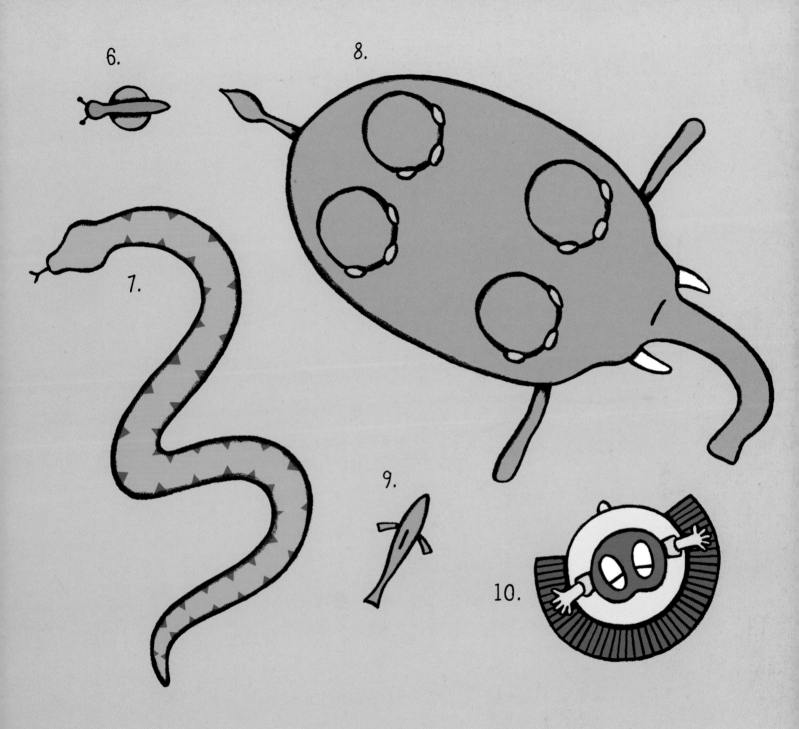

No Way!

"I know a secret," said Daisy to her best friend Gabby.

"Tell me it," said Gabby.

"No way," said Daisy.

"Please tell me," said Gabby.

"Not for all the treasure in all the treasure chests on all the treasure islands in the world," said Daisy.

"Please tell me," said Gabby.

"Not for all the snowballs in all the snow on all the mountain tops in the world," said Daisy.

"Please tell me," said Gabby.

"Not for all the shells on all the beaches at all the seasides in the world," said Daisy.

"Please, please tell me," said Gabby.

"Not for all the white rabbits in all the black hats on all the magicians' heads in the world," said Daisy.

"Please, please, please tell me," said Gabby.

"Not for all the squirty string in all the clowns' pockets in all the circuses in the world," said Daisy.

"Tell me, tell me, tell me!" said Gabby.

"No way, no way, no way!" said Daisy.

"If you tell me, I'll give you a piece of my chewing gum," said Gabby.

"OK," said Daisy.

Gabby handed Daisy a piece of her chewing gum and waited while Daisy chewed. And chewed and chewed and chewed.

"Well?" said Gabby impatiently. "Tell me the secret!"

Daisy stopped chewing and lowered her voice.

"Well . . . Jamie says that Jack says that Elliott says that Lauren says that Jasmine says that Ben says that Connor says that Jordan says that Hannah . . .

. . . is getting a guinea pig for her birthday."

"Give me my chewing gum back!" said Gabby, stamping her foot crossly.

"Why?" asked Daisy in mid-chew.

"I told Jordan that in the first place!" said Gabby.

Daisy's Guide to Puddles

Puddles happen when it rains.

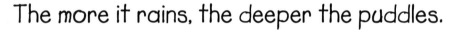

The more it rains, the deeper the puddles.

The best puddles are deep puddles.

But not TOO deep puddles.

Puddles are for splashing in!

The higher *you jump*, the bigger the splash.

SPLASH!

If you don't want to get your socks wet, wear wellies.

If you do want to get your socks wet, wear jellies.

Puddles aren't always wet. Sometimes they are frozen.
When it is very cold the wet turns to ice.

You can crunch the ice with your feet!
The harder you stamp,
the bigger the crunch!

CRUNCH!

If the ice is very thick
you can do skids!

All puddles are great!
Well, nearly all puddles.

Whatnots and Whatsits

The whatnot with the rubbish in it is a skip.

The thingy on that car is a caravan.

The doodahs in the road are traffic cones.

The whatsit on that
bike is a padlock.

The wosname on that house
is called a satellite dish.

The wosnames in that
field are called hay bales.

The thingy on that
sign is an ibex.

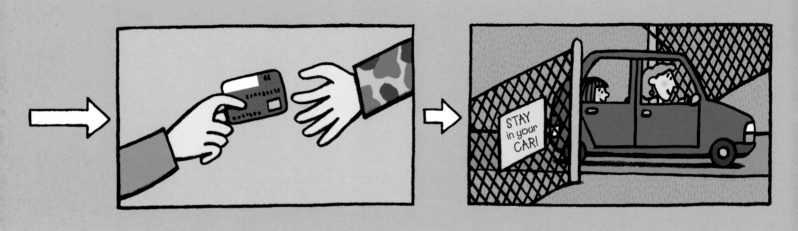

The whatnot Mum is paying with is a credit card.

The wosname that we're driving through is an electric fence.

The wosname that he's pulling off is our aerial.

The whatsits he's chewing are our windscreen wipers.

The wosname over there is a jaguar.

The thingy on our car is a baboon.

The words that Mum is saying are unrepeatable!

Bubbles

I like blowing bubbles! Can you find
my mouse, my bracelet, my snowman,
my worm, my lolly, my funny face . . .

. . . my Tyrannosaurus rex
riding a bicycle . . .
Oh, no! He's just
POPPED!

See you in the
next Daisy book!

Find out more about Daisy!

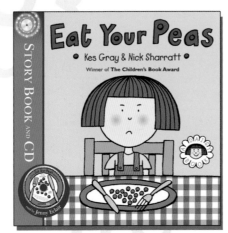

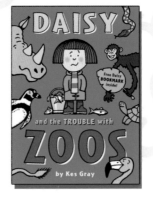

New longer Daisy story books!

Come and play with Daisy at www.daisyclub.co.uk